Suni Lee

Grace Hansen

Abdo Kids
OLYMPIC BIOGRAPHIES
Kids

Abdo Kids Jumbo is an Imprint of Abdo Kids
abdobooks.com

abdobooks.com

Published by Abdo Kids, a division of ABDO, P.O. Box 398166, Minneapolis, Minnesota 55439.

Abdo Kids Jumbo™ is a trademark and logo of Abdo Kids.

Printed in the United States of America, North Mankato, Minnesota.

102021

012022

THIS BOOK CONTAINS RECYCLED MATERIALS

Photo Credits: AP Images, Getty Images, iStock, Shutterstock

Production Contributors: Teddy Borth, Jennie Forsberg, Grace Hansen
Design Contributors: Candice Keimig, Pakou Moua

Library of Congress Control Number: 2021944663

Publisher's Cataloging-in-Publication Data

Names: Hansen, Grace, author.

Title: Suni Lee / by Grace Hansen

Description: Minneapolis, Minnesota : Abdo Kids, 2022 | Series: Olympic biographies | Includes online resources and index.

Identifiers: ISBN 9781098261429 (lib. bdg.) | ISBN 9781098261481 (ebook) | ISBN 9781098261511 (Read-to-me ebook)

Subjects: LCSH: Lee, Sunisa, 2003---Juvenile literature. | Gymnastics--Juvenile literature. | Women gymnasts--Juvenile literature. | Women Olympic athletes--Juvenile literature. | Hmong American women--Juvenile literature. | Asian American athletes--Juvenile literature.

Classification: DDC 796.44092--dc23

Table of Contents

Early Years

Sunisa "Suni" Lee was born on March 9, 2003. She grew up in St. Paul, Minnesota.

Minnesota
St. Paul

Suni watched videos of gymnasts like Nastia Liukin and Shawn Johnson. She thought gymnastics looked like fun.

Shawn Johnson

Suni was just 6 when she started practicing gymnastics. She began competing at age 7. That year, she won the **all-around** at a state meet.

Suni kept getting better and better. By age 11, she had made it to the **elite** level.

World Competitor

Suni attended the 2019 World Artistic Gymnastics Championships. She was the youngest competitor.

Suni earned a bronze medal on the uneven bars. She also won silver in the **floor exercise**! Suni and Team USA took home the gold!

USA

Tokyo!

In June 2021, Suni competed in the US National Gymnastics Championships. Her performance earned her a spot at the **Olympic Trials**. Suni did very well there. She qualified for the 2020 Olympics in Tokyo, Japan!

U.S. OLYMPIC
TEAM TRIALS
GYMNASTICS

In Tokyo, Suni helped her team **clinch** silver. In the individual **all-around**, Suni hit all four of her routines. She got the highest score on the uneven bars. She won the gold!

Super Suni

Suni is an amazing gymnast. She is also a history maker! Suni is the first Hmong-American Olympian.

HMOOB
SAINT PAUL
FIRE

More Facts

- Suni took home three medals at the 2020 Olympics. She earned gold in the **all-around**, silver in team, and bronze on the uneven bars. She also got 5th place on beam!
- Suni's father, John, was in a tragic accident in 2019. It caused him to become **paralyzed**. On harder days, he thinks of Suni. He said, "When I get angry at myself, I look at Sunisa and think about what she has had to go through to get where she's at, and she inspires me."
- Suni's family could not attend the Olympics due to the COVID-19 pandemic. So, her friends and family had a watch party. They cheered her on from Minnesota!

Glossary

all-around – all four events in women's gymnastics, including the vault, uneven bars, balance beam, and floor exercise.

clinch – to make certain or final.

elite – in gymnastics, the 11th level of competition made up of truly dedicated athletes.

floor exercise – a gymnastics event that can include tumbling lines, dance elements, turns, and leaps. It is performed to music in a 40 square foot (3.7 sq m) area and lasts 70 to 90 seconds.

Olympic Trials – competitions held in certain sports to select the United States' participants in those sports at the Olympic Games.

paralyzed – unable to move some or all areas of the body.

Index